This book is a work of fiction. Any references to historical events, real people, or real places are used fictitiously. Other names, characters, places, and events are products of the author's imagination, and any resemblance to actual events or places or persons, living or dead, is entirely coincidental.

LITTLE SIMON
An imprint of Simon & Schuster Children's Publishing Division • 1230 Avenue of the Americas, New York, New York 10020 • First Little Simon paperback edition April 2021 • Copyright © 2021 by Simon & Schuster, Inc. All rights reserved, including the right of reproduction in whole or in part in any form. LITTLE SIMON is a registered trademark of Simon & Schuster, Inc., and associated colophon is a trademark of Simon & Schuster, Inc. For information about special discounts for bulk purchases, please contact Simon & Schuster Special Sales at 1-866-506-1949 or business@simonandschuster.com. The Simon & Schuster Speakers Bureau can bring authors to your live event. For more information or to book an event contact the Simon & Schuster Speakers Bureau at 1-866-248-3049 or visit our website at www.simonspeakers.com.
Series designed by Laura Roode.
Book designed by Hannah Frece. The text of this book was set in Usherwood.
Manufactured in the United States of America 0321 MTN 10 9 8 7 6 5 4 3 2 1
Cataloging-in-Publication Data is available for this title from the Library of Congress.
ISBN 978-1-5344-8163-3 (hc)
ISBN 978-1-5344-8162-6 (pbk)
ISBN 978-1-5344-8164-0 (eBook)

the adventures of
SOPHIE MOUSE

(17)

The Ladybug Party

By Poppy Green • Illustrated by Jennifer A. Bell

LITTLE SIMON

New York London Toronto Syd____ ___ ___hi

Contents

chapter 1

Artist's Block

Sophie Mouse stared at the blank white canvas on her easel. She had artist's block. She didn't know what to paint.

Silverlake Elementary School was closed for spring break. Sophie and her little brother, Winston, had been home for a week already.

Sophie had painted a lot at first. She did portraits of her mom and dad. She painted Winston splashing at Forget-Me-Not Lake. She did a whole series of close-up wildflower paintings. She painted the view out her bedroom window: sunrises, sunsets, rainy days, sunny days.

But she hadn't painted anything for the past few days. She had run out of ideas.

Sophie trudged down the stairs of the Mouse family's cottage, which was nestled in the roots of a big oak tree. She opened the front door. Outside, the morning sun shone through the dew-covered blades of grass. The light rays made rainbows inside each dewdrop.

Sophie was already dressed. She'd had breakfast. She decided not to waste such a beautiful morning.

"I'm going for a walk!" she said to her mom and dad in the kitchen. They waved as they nibbled on their breakfast.

Then Sophie grabbed her artist's 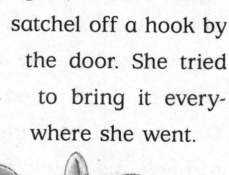 satchel off a hook by the door. She tried to bring it everywhere she went.

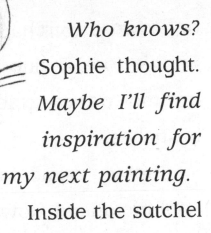

Who knows?
Sophie thought.
Maybe I'll find
inspiration for
my next painting.

Inside the satchel were tins of paint, paintbrushes, scrap paper, and empty cloth pouches. Sophie used the pouches to collect flowers, berries—anything she could use to make a new color of paint.

The morning air felt cool and refreshing as Sophie walked through the forest. She passed the playground Winston loved so much. She walked on toward Birch Tree Slide. Then Sophie took a side path that wound around to the tunnel of honeysuckle branches.

Sophie came around a bend. Looking ahead, down a long straight-away, she saw a blur of red.

What was that?

It was a beautiful color. Darker

red than her poppy red paint. But brighter than pomegranate red. Sophie picked up her pace, trying to get closer.

There it was again! The red blur was farther away this time. Whatever it was, it was moving very fast. Sophie broke into a jog. But she didn't seem to be catching up.

Then Sophie had an idea. Maybe she could blaze a shortcut through the brush. She could skip the next bend and come out farther along the path.

Sure enough, Sophie did come out onto a path. But was it the same path, or a different one? She caught a glimpse of red through the greenery ahead! Sophie sniffed the air. That direction smelled like due north. Her nose would keep her on track.

Sophie darted through ferns and grass. Finally, she pushed a low branch aside and came out into a clearing.

She stopped in her tracks and blinked.

Sophie couldn't believe her eyes.

chapter 2

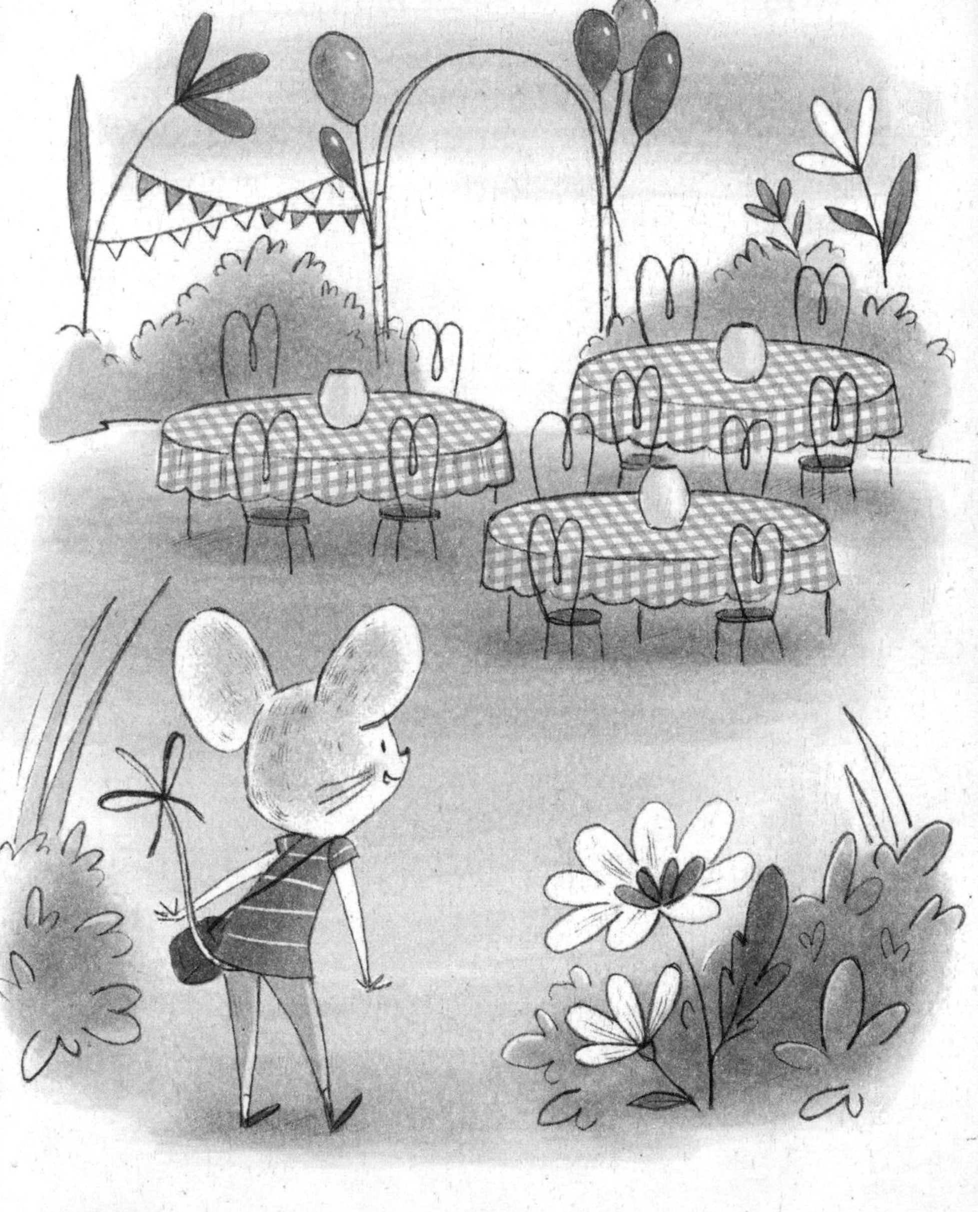

The Ladybug's Surprise

Sophie was in a beautiful green clearing. Small bushes surrounded the area.

And right in the middle of it were groupings of round tables and chairs. A garden trellis was decorated with red balloons. It looked like a setup for a grand party.

But there wasn't any party going

on. There was just one very busy
ladybug, rushing to and fro.

A ladybug! thought Sophie. *She
must have been the red blur!*

The ladybug didn't seem to notice
Sophie. She was too busy putting
tablecloths on the tables. As Sophie
moved closer, she could hear the
ladybug talking to herself as she
worked.

"I have to wash the napkins tonight. And iron them. Then fold them. Oh, I can't forget the cake! And the lemonade."

Just then the ladybug turned. She saw Sophie and jumped.

"My word!" the ladybug said with a laugh. "You gave me quite the scare!"

"I'm sorry," Sophie said. "I didn't mean to scare you!" She introduced herself.

"Very nice to meet you," the ladybug replied. "I'm Clara Ladybug." She explained that she was throwing a surprise party for her grandmother. "It's tomorrow at noon. And I have so much more to do before then."

Sophie looked around. "Everything looks so nice already," she said. There were red-and-white checkered tablecloths, a stack of blue napkins, and pink flower vases. "I love all the colors you've chosen," Sophie added.

"Thank you!" replied Clara. "My favorite color is red. That's why I chose red balloons. My sister's favorite color is blue. And for the guest of honor, my grandmother, we'll have a yellow cake. Her favorite color is yellow!"

Clara sighed. Her smile faded from her face.

"It's been wonderful to chat," she said to Sophie. "But I have to get back to work. I need to organize all the food, pick up the cake, order the surprise banner, get the punch bowl—"

Sophie interrupted. "That sounds like too much to do yourself!"

Clara shrugged. "I don't want to tell too many others, you see. I want the guests to be surprised by some of the details."

Sophie grinned. "Well, I know someone who could help," she said. "And she already knows all the details."

The ladybug's face lit up. "Really?"
she said. "Who?"

"Me!" Sophie exclaimed.

~ chapter 3 ~

Sophie Lends a Hand

"Are you sure?" Clara asked. "I mean, if you could run some errands for me, I *could* keep working on the setup. That would save me so much time!"

Sophie nodded enthusiastically. "Of course!"

Clara clutched Sophie's paw. "Oh, thank you! Thank you so much!"

She listed the errands for Sophie.

"First, could you go to the bakery? I need to change the order for the vanilla sheet cake from pink frosting to yellow," Clara said. "And if you could pick up some purple flowers, that would be so helpful!"

Clara also asked Sophie to deliver a message to Mr. Handy at Handy's Hardware. She needed a banner that said WELCOME HOME, GRANDMA!

"Oh!" Clara added. "And the cake should say the same thing too!" Clara's brow furrowed as if she was trying to remember something. "I think I told the baker about that already, though." Then her expression softened. "She's the best baker in town. I hear she even won a Year's Best Baker award. In fact, she's a mouse just like you!"

Sophie smiled. "I know exactly who you mean," she said. And she knew exactly where to find her. At home! Sophie's mom owned the bakery in Pine Needle Grove. And Sophie had actually helped her mom win the Year's Best Baker award!

"I can take care of all those things. I'll bring them here in time for the party tomorrow," Sophie assured Clara.

Clara was so grateful.

"Wait!" Clara said. "I think I have a pen and paper here somewhere." She started looking around a pile on the table. She reached into the pockets of her apron. "I can write this all down for you if I can just find a pen."

"That's okay!" Sophie reassured Clara. "I can file it all away up here." She tapped the side of her head. *After all*, thought Sophie, *I'm an artist with an eye for detail. I'm sure I can remember the list.*

Sophie said goodbye and headed off, excited to help her new friend.

She went back through the brush, found the path, and hurried toward home. Sophie was nearly there when she met a familiar frog and snake coming from the other direction.

"Sophie!" Hattie Frog called. "We just stopped at your house. Your mom said you were out for a walk."

29

"We're on our way to Butterfly Brook," Owen Snake added. "Want to come?"

Sophie excitedly told them about Clara and the surprise party—and her top-secret errands. "But you can't tell anyone," Sophie said.

Hattie and Owen promised they wouldn't.

Hattie looked at Owen. "Are you thinking what I'm thinking?" she asked him. "This sounds like more fun than Butterfly Brook."

Owen nodded. "Can we help?" he asked Sophie.

Sophie clapped. This was going to be even more fun with her friends along!

chapter 4

Color Mix-Up

Sophie led her friends back toward her house. She wanted to ask her mom about the cake.

On the way, she told Hattie and Owen about the stops they had to make after that. "We need to place an order for a banner saying WELCOME HOME, GRANDMA! Then we need to get some flowers."

Owen nodded.

"Got it," said Hattie.

At Sophie's house, Lily Mouse was putting on her apron. The counter was crowded with bowls, utensils, and ingredients. A big bowl of pink

frosting sat next to a large vanilla
sheet cake. Sophie spied a small piece
of paper next to the cake. On it, Lily
Mouse had written CLARA LADYBUG.

"Mom, guess who I just met!" Sophie blurted out.

"Hmm," Lily Mouse said distractedly. She was staring at a recipe card. "I'd love to guess. But maybe later. Right now I need to get a cake frosted for a very important order."

Sophie grinned. "I know! A cake
for a surprise party tomorrow. Right?"

That got her mom's attention. She
looked at Sophie with wide eyes.
"How did you know?" Lily asked.

Sophie told her about meeting Clara. "I said I could run a few errands for her. She asked me to speak to the baker about the cake," Sophie said with a laugh. "Can you please change the frosting color from pink to yellow?"

"Oh, sure!" Lily Mouse replied. "I can use this pink frosting for a batch of strawberry cupcakes."

Sophie thanked her. Then she rushed off with Hattie and Owen to their next stop.

On their way to town, the friends chatted about their spring breaks so far.

Owen had been swimming almost every day. "Yesterday I stayed in the water too long and my tail turned blue. I'm cold-blooded, you know."

Hattie's dad had given her a little part of the garden to tend. She could plant whatever she wanted. "So far I've planted purple pansies, yellow daylilies, and bright pink peonies," Hattie said proudly.

Sophie told her friends about all the paintings she'd made. She listed some of her new paint colors: petunia pink and tangerine orange.

"That reminds me," Owen said. "Did either of you see last night's sunset?"

"Yes!" Hattie exclaimed. "The clouds were streaked with red and orange."

Sophie smiled. It sounded like her artist's eye was rubbing off on her friends!

Soon they arrived in Pine Needle Grove. "Now," said Sophie, "maybe we can split up. I can go order the banner. Could you two get the flowers?"

Owen nodded. "What color?" he asked.

Sophie opened her mouth to answer. But nothing came out.

Her mind was a swirl of colors from all the talk of sunsets and flower gardens and paint colors. Sophie closed her eyes and tried to remember Clara's instructions.

She saw red and orange clouds . . .
bright pink peonies . . . a purple
cake. Wait, no. It was a yellow cake!
So was it a purple banner? And red
flowers?

"Oh no!" said Sophie. "I can't
remember!"

chapter 5

Welcome Home?

Sophie looked to Hattie and Owen for help. "Do you remember?" she asked them. "What did I say when I was telling you what we had to do?"

Owen and Hattie looked at each other, then back at Sophie. They both shrugged.

"You said a banner and some flowers," Hattie said.

"But what color flowers?" Sophie asked.

Owen shook his head. "You didn't say."

Sophie moaned. Oh, why didn't she mention the color? Then her friends could have helped her remember.

Sophie wracked her brain. Clara had definitely said *her* favorite color was red. That's why the balloons were red. Were the flowers supposed to match the red balloons? Sophie didn't think so.

Just then, Sophie spied a pink rib-
bon in the bookstore window display.
Pink? she wondered. Yes, Sophie
remembered there *was* something
pink for the party setup. Maybe that
was it. It had to be.

"Pink flowers!" Sophie told Hattie
and Owen. "I'm almost positive."

"Okay!" Hattie said. "We will take care of it!" She and Owen hurried off to the florist's shop.

Meanwhile, Sophie headed over to Handy's Hardware to order the banner.

A bell jingled as Sophie pushed open the front door and stepped inside. But the bell was nothing compared to the loud sounds of hammers pounding wood. Mr. Handy was

standing at a workbench. He was supervising a troop of Junior Forest Scouts. It looked to Sophie like one of Mr. Handy's carpentry workshops. They were making picture frames.

"Excuse me, Mr. Handy!" Sophie called out.

Mr. Handy turned and waved hello. "Didn't hear you come in!" he shouted over the noise. "What can I do for you?"

Sophie took a deep breath. "I need to—" *Bang! Bang!* "I need to order—" *Bang!*

Sophie started and restarted the sentence, speeding up each time. Finally, she got it all out between

hammer strokes. "I need to order a banner that says WELCOME HOME, GRANDMA!"

Mr. Handy nodded. "Okay!" *Bang!* "When do you need it?" he bellowed.

"Can it be ready tomorrow morning?" Sophie yelled back. *Bang! Bang!*

Mr. Handy pulled a note pad and pencil out of his work apron. He scribbled something down. Then

he smiled at Sophie. "It'll be ready!" he shouted. *Bang, bang, bang!*

"Thank you!" Sophie shouted. She turned to go.

But as Sophie got to the door, Mr. Handy called after her. "Was that 'Happy Birthday, Grandpa'?" *Bang, bang!*

Sophie shook her head. "Not Grandpa." *Bang!* "Grandma!"

Mr. Handy nodded. "Got it!" he shouted.

"See you tomorrow!"

Outside, Sophie met up with Hattie and Owen. Hattie was holding a big bunch of pink flowers wrapped in florist's paper. She handed them to Sophie.

"What do you think?" Owen asked Sophie.

"They're beautiful," she replied. *Yes,* thought Sophie. *Clara had said pink.*

Hadn't she?

— chapter 6 —

Hattie and Her Purple Pansies

The next day, Sophie woke up early. The surprise party was at noon. Sophie wanted to deliver everything Clara needed in plenty of time.

Sophie headed downstairs. Winston was eating his cereal at the counter. He watched his mom scoop icing into a piping bag. A big cake box sat open, with the frosted yellow cake inside. It looked like she was getting ready to write the message on the cake.

"Wow, Mom!" Sophie said. "The frosting looks amazing." On the sides, her mom had used a frosting pattern called basket weave. "You are so good at that."

Mrs. Mouse beamed. "Thank you, Sophie," she said.

Sophie poured herself some cereal. She ate it in a flash. Then she announced she was going to pick up the banner.

"By the time you get back, the cake will be all done," her mom replied.

"Great!" said Sophie.

She speed-walked the whole way to Handy's Hardware. She couldn't wait to deliver everything to Clara!

Mr. Handy was in the middle of another workshop. It was the same troop of Junior Forest Scouts. Luckily, today they were painting the picture frames they'd made. So it wasn't nearly as noisy.

Even so, Sophie was glad to see the banner was all rolled up and ready for pickup.

Banner in hand, Sophie hurried home to get the cake and flowers. Everything was coming together! She daydreamed about how it would all look. The red balloons. The yellow cake. The blue napkins. The purple flowers.

Oh no! Not pink. Purple!

All of a sudden, Sophie knew. She was supposed to get purple flowers!

She regretted not writing everything down, as Clara had suggested. It was just too many colors to keep track of!

Sophie was more than halfway home. She stood frozen on the path, not sure which way to go. Turn back

to town? Was there time to get to the florist for purple flowers? Or continue home, and at least bring Clara the cake and banner? Sophie looked up at the sun. What time was it? Clara was counting on her.

Sophie's stomach was in knots!

Just ahead was the turnoff to Hattie's house. Maybe she'd know what to do. Sophie scurried along the path. Before long, she came to the stream bank and Hattie's house. Half of it was built into the bank. Half of it floated on the water.

Sophie knocked loudly on the front door. Hattie answered.

"I'm so glad you're here!" Sophie cried. She confessed her flower mistake. "I was supposed to get purple ones. I feel terrible!"

Hattie patted her on the back reassuringly. "Oh, Sophie, it's okay. Everyone makes mistakes."

Sophie sighed. "I know, but—"

"Besides," Hattie went on, "I have plenty of purple flowers growing in my garden. Remember?"

Sophie shook her head. "Oh no, Hattie," she said. "I couldn't take your pansies."

"Yes, you can!" Hattie cried. "You

should! I would be honored for my
flowers to decorate the party!"

chapter 7

Not Quite Right

Later that day, Hattie and Owen helped Sophie carry everything to the grassy clearing.

Clara was there, setting out all the food for the party. She was so excited to see Sophie that she fluttered her wings a few times.

Sophie introduced Clara to Owen and Hattie. "They helped me get everything for the party," Sophie said.

"I hope you don't mind. I let them in on the secret. They didn't tell anyone."

"Of course," Clara replied. "Thank you—all three of you—for your help."

"Everything looks great!" Owen said, glancing around.

Owen was right. Since yesterday, Clara had set all the tables. A buffet table held platters of delicious-looking sandwiches. A punch bowl was filled with what looked like lemonade.

"Yes, I think I'm just about ready," Clara said. She pointed to the box in Sophie's hands. "Ooh, is that the cake?"

Sophie placed the box on a table and opened the lid. Clara gasped in delight at Lily Mouse's creation. The piped writing on top of the yellow frosting was in steady, even cursive.

"It's perfect!" Clara cried. "And I can't wait to taste it!"

Hattie inched forward to present the flowers. "Sophie said you wanted purple?" Hattie said shyly. She sometimes needed a minute to warm up to strangers.

"Pansies!" Clara exclaimed. "Those are my grandmother's favorite!"

Sophie had to give Hattie full credit. "They're from Hattie's own garden." Sophie then explained that she'd gotten confused about the flower color.

Owen was holding the pink flowers from the florist. "So we brought pink flowers, too," he said.

Clara clapped. "You can never have too many flowers!" she said.

Then Sophie pulled out the banner, which was

tucked under her arm. She handed
it to Clara. "Last but not least . . ."

Clara unrolled it and read it out
loud. "'Happy Birthday, Grandma'? Hm."

Sophie frowned. "Wait. What?"
She came around to the front side
of the banner. "Oh no!" she said with

a groan. "'Happy Birthday'? How did that happen?" Hadn't she ordered the banner to say WELCOME HOME, GRANDMA? Mr. Handy had even written it down. How had it turned out so wrong?

Then Sophie remembered the Junior Forest Scouts in the store. All the hammering!

"Clara, I'm so sorry!" Sophie said. "What can I do? Maybe I can fix it."

Sophie couldn't believe it. First the

flowers. And now she had messed up *again*!

Sophie could see Clara was disappointed. But she was too kind to say so.

"Sophie, do not worry," Clara said. "You've already helped me so much. The banner is really not important. And the party is starting soon. Guests will be arriving in ten, maybe fifteen minutes."

But Sophie wasn't giving up.

chapter 8

Sophie Gets to Work

"Hattie, Owen," Sophie said to her friends. "Will you help me?"

"Yes!" Owen said right away.

"Of course," Hattie replied. "But . . . what's the plan, Sophie?"

With a twinkle in her eye, Sophie patted her artist's satchel. Hattie and Owen nodded. Sophie was always prepared to paint.

Sophie picked up the banner. "I have to give it a try," Sophie told Clara. "And if it's not done in time, at least I tried. Right?"

Clara nodded. "Okay!" she said. "Is there anything I can do?"

Sophie thought for a moment. "I'll need water," she said. "Do you have any?"

Clara frowned. "I don't," she said. "But there's a stream on the other side of those bushes!" Clara flew off.

A minute later, she flew back. She had used one of the party cups to collect water. She gave it to Sophie.

"Thank you!" Sophie cried. She turned to Owen and Hattie. "Follow me!"

Sophie led them to the far end of the clearing. Clara stayed behind and waited for the first guests.

"Okay," said Sophie. She unrolled the banner in the grass. She put down the cup of water. She pulled her paint tins out of her satchel. "Let me see what I can do."

Hattie and Owen looked a little skeptical.

"Sophie," Owen said, "that lettering is pretty dark and bold. Won't

it be hard to turn 'Happy Birthday'
into 'Welcome Home'?"

Sophie laughed. "Yes, that would
be hard," she said. "But that's not
what I'm doing."

Sophie flipped the banner over. It
was blank on the other side.

"I'm starting from scratch!" she announced.

Hattie and Owen looked at each other and smiled. They knew what Sophie could do with a blank canvas and paint.

The next ten minutes were a blur.

A swirl of paint mixing. A flurry of brushstrokes. A wash of water for cleaning brushes.

Sophie used her darkest color, indigo ink, for the message. Lettering wasn't her strongest skill. But Sophie was inspired by her mom's lettering on the cake. Steady, even cursive.

She tried to make it look just like Lily Mouse's.

When that was done, Sophie looked over to see that some of the party guests had arrived. But no sign of Clara's grandmother yet.

So Sophie decided to paint a little more.

She used her new color, honey-dew green, for painting the greenery. Periwinkle purple was just right for the flower petals. She used butter-cup yellow for the cake.

And she mixed a special new shade of red for the balloons. "I think I'll call it ladybug red," Sophie said.

By now many more guests had arrived.

"Sophie," said Owen, "I think you might be out of time."

Sophie nodded and stepped back from her work. She looked at her friends.

"Be honest," she said. "What do you think?"

Hattie smiled and opened her mouth to say something.

But just then, they heard Clara's voice from across the glen. It was hushed but clear. "Here she comes!"

chapter 9

SURPRISE!

Sophie grabbed one end of the banner. Hattie grabbed the other. Owen carried the middle by holding the top edge in his mouth.

Together they sprinted across the clearing.

One by one, party guests turned to look at them. A murmur of voices rippled through the crowd.

"Who?"

"What is it?"

"What does it say?"

As Sophie, Hattie, and Owen got close, the guests could read the message. Their puzzled faces brightened and broke into smiles. In the center of the crowd, Clara turned and saw the banner. Her

mouth dropped open in surprise.

Then Clara locked eyes with Sophie. She smiled and mouthed two words. *Thank you.*

"I think she likes it," Owen said to Sophie.

Sophie nodded. She thought so too.

Then, at the sound of a twig snap-
ping, all heads turned the other way.

A well-dressed, older ladybug
emerged from the forest path. She
was flying over.

At her side was a young ladybug.
"Just a little farther, Grandma," the
little ladybug was saying.

"Where are we going again?" Grandma Ladybug said. "I thought you said—"

Grandma Ladybug looked up and stopped in her tracks.

"SURPRISE!" the guests shouted all together.

The older ladybug stood speechless, taking it all in. The familiar faces of her loved ones. The balloons. The flowers. The food. The tables and chairs.

And in the back, held up high by a mouse, a frog, and a snake, was a colorful, artfully painted banner. It told Grandma Ladybug loud and clear why they were all there.

Welcome Home, Grandma!

Oh, Grandma Ladybug looked surprised, all right. Surprised and very, very happy.

Sophie breathed a sigh of relief. She had done it. She had fixed the banner. And just in the nick of time.

Grandma made the rounds, greeting all the guests. While all eyes were on her, Sophie, Hattie, and Owen found two long sticks. They tied the banner to the sticks. Then they planted the sticks in the ground.

Now the banner sat perfectly over the balloon trellis.

Sophie cleaned her hands on her
skirt. "I think our work here is done!"
she said to Hattie and Owen.

She packed up, and slung her
satchel over her shoulder. Then the
three friends made a quiet exit down
the forest path. They wanted to leave
Clara to enjoy the party.

But as they snuck away, Sophie felt a tap on her shoulder. She turned. Clara had come after them.

"You're not leaving, are you?" Clara asked. "Oh, please stay. You have to meet Grandma! I'm going to tell her this party would not have happened without you."

So Sophie, Hattie, and Owen happily agreed to stay.

As they walked back into the clearing, Clara pulled Sophie aside. "And my grandmother especially wanted to meet the creator of that beautiful banner!"

Sophie beamed proudly.

chapter 10

Goodbye, Artist's Block!

Later that night, Sophie climbed into bed. She was so tired. From the panic over the flowers to the speed-painting of the banner, it had been a long day.

And that was before the party had even started! Sophie, Hattie, and Owen had stayed until the sun went

down. Ladybugs really knew how to throw a party! Sophie wondered if they were still there, celebrating Grandma Ladybug. Even now, under the stars.

Sophie didn't want to forget her favorite moments from the party. But she'd had enough of painting for one day. So she got out her sketchbook and pencils.

She sat up in bed and sketched Clara hugging her grandmother right after the big surprise.

She drew Clara's grandmother blowing out the candles on her yellow cake.

She sketched the balloons on the trellis and her custom, hand-painted banner.

She sketched Hattie holding her beautiful pansies.

Finally, Sophie sketched herself with her two best friends and her newest friend, Clara.

Then Sophie tucked her sketch-book underneath her pillow. She turned out her light.

As she drifted off to sleep, Sophie smiled. *Take that, artist's block!* She now had a whole sketchbook full of ideas for paintings. *That* would keep her busy.

If not for the rest of break, then at least for a few days.

The End

the adventures of

SOPHiE MOUSE

For excerpts, activities, and more about
these adorable tales & tails, visit
AdventuresofSophieMouse.com!

If you like Sophie Mouse, you'll love

the CRiTTeR club